Dandy Dogs

Mary Elizabeth Salzmann
AUTHOR

C.A. Nobens
ILLUSTRATOR

Consulting Editor, Diane Craig, M.A./Reading Specialist

ABDO
Publishing Company

Published by ABDO Publishing Company, 4940 Viking Drive, Edina, Minnesota 55435.

Copyright © 2007 by Abdo Consulting Group, Inc. International copyrights reserved in all countries. No part of this book may be reproduced in any form without written permission from the publisher. SandCastle™ is a trademark and logo of ABDO Publishing Company.

Printed in the United States.

CREDITS

Edited by: Pam Price

Concept Development: Nancy Tuminelly

Cover and Interior Design and Production: Mighty Media

Photo Credits: Blend Images, JupiterImages Corporation, Labat Jean-Michel/PHONE/Peter Arnold, Inc., Labat & Rouquette/PHONE/BIOS/Peter Arnold, Inc., Photodisc, ShutterStock

LIBRARY OF CONGRESS CATALOGING-IN-PUBLICATION DATA

Salzmann, Mary Elizabeth, 1968-
  Dandy dogs / Mary Elizabeth Salzmann ; illustrated by C.A. Nobens.
     p. cm. -- (Perfect pets)
  ISBN-13: 978-1-59928-746-1
  ISBN-10: 1-59928-746-3
  1. Dogs--Juvenile literature. I. Nobens, C. A., ill. II. Title.

SF426.5.S24 2007
636.7--dc22
                            2006033249

SandCastle™ books are created by a professional team of educators, reading specialists, and content developers around five essential components—phonemic awareness, phonics, vocabulary, text comprehension, and fluency—to assist young readers as they develop reading skills and strategies and increase their general knowledge. All books are written, reviewed, and leveled for guided reading, early reading intervention, and Accelerated Reader® programs for use in shared, guided, and independent reading and writing activities to support a balanced approach to literacy instruction.

SandCastle Level: Transitional

LET US KNOW

SandCastle would like to hear your stories about reading this book. What is your favorite page? Was there something hard that you needed help with? Share the ups and downs of learning to read. We want to hear from you! To get posted on the ABDO Publishing Company Web site, send us e-mail at:

sandcastle@abdopublishing.com

DOGS

Dogs are friendly, loyal, playful, and protective. Many people think they make dandy pets!

Elijah likes to walk his dog in the woods. Dogs need exercise to stay fit.

Allison feeds her dog every day. She also makes sure her dog has fresh water.

Makayla brushes her dog. Brushing keeps her dog's fur clean and shiny.

Nicole teaches her dog to come, sit, and stay. It is important for dogs to obey their owners.

Carlos takes his dog to the veterinarian for a checkup. The vet lets Carlos listen to his dog's heart.

A Dog Story

Mark takes his dog Lark down the street to the dog park.

Mark removes Lark's leash when she sits. The first dog they see is little Fritz.

Mark brings a ball
for Lark to chase.
Sometimes it
becomes a race!

Lark is the first
to get the ball,
just before
it hits the wall.

Lark runs with all
the other dogs.
They dash around trees
and jump over logs.

Then Lark finds a stick.
She plays tug with a
dog named Mick.

Mark calls Lark,
and she comes in a blink.
She is thirsty,
so he gives her a drink.

Mark says, "You're a
dandy dog, Lark!
Now let's go home
before it gets dark."

Fun facts

Dogs have existed for more than 12,000 years.

Dogs have about 200 million more scent receptors then people do.

There are more than 400 different breeds of dogs.

Basset hounds are the slowest breed of dog. Greyhounds are the fastest.

The Irish wolfhound is the tallest breed of dog. The English mastiff is the heaviest breed of dog. The Chihuahua is the smallest breed in height and weight.

Glossary

blink – a very short amount of time.

dandy – very good or excellent.

fit – healthy and in good physical shape.

loyal – faithful or devoted to someone or something.

obey – to follow rules, orders, or directions.

protective – the act of guarding someone or something from harm or danger.

shiny – bright and glossy.

veterinarian – a doctor who takes care of animals.

About SandCastle™

A professional team of educators, reading specialists, and content developers created the SandCastle™ series to support young readers as they develop reading skills and strategies and increase their general knowledge. The SandCastle™ series has four levels that correspond to early literacy development in young children. The levels are provided to help teachers and parents select appropriate books for young readers.

Emerging Readers
(no flags)

Beginning Readers
(1 flag)

Transitional Readers
(2 flags)

Fluent Readers
(3 flags)

These levels are meant only as a guide. All levels are subject to change.

To see a complete list of SandCastle™ books and other nonfiction titles from ABDO Publishing Company, visit **www.abdopublishing.com** or contact us at:
4940 Viking Drive, Edina, Minnesota 55435 • 1-800-800-1312 • fax: 1-952-831-1632